The SLEEPY MEN
MARGARET WISE BROWN

ILLUSTRATED BY
ROBERT RAYEVSKY

Hyperion Books for Children
New York

To my son Rafi
— R. R.

Printed in Hong Kong by
South China Printing Company (1988) Ltd.
FIRST EDITION
1 3 5 7 9 10 8 6 4 2

The artwork for each picture is prepared using acrylic and ink.
This book is set in 16-point Antique Olive Roman.

Library of Congress Cataloging-in-Publication Data
Brown, Margaret Wise, date.
The sleepy men / Margaret Wise Brown ;
illustrated by Robert Rayevsky —
1st ed.
    p.   cm.
Summary: After a big sleepy man tells a little sleepy man a story
about the Man in the Moon, they both fall asleep.
ISBN 0-7868-0154-9 (trade) — ISBN 0-7868-2126-4 (lib. bdg.)
[1. Sleep—Fiction.
2. Moon—Fiction.]
I. Rayevsky, Robert,
ill. II. Title.
PZ7.B8163S1   1996
[E]—dc20   94-41939

There was a **big** sleepy man

and a LITTLE sleepy man.

The **big** sleepy man yawned a great big yawn

and the **LITTLE** sleepy man yawned a sleepy little yawn.

Then the big sleepy man gave a great big stretch

and the little sleepy man gave a little sleepy stretch.

Then the big sleepy man got into bed

and the little sleepy man got into bed.

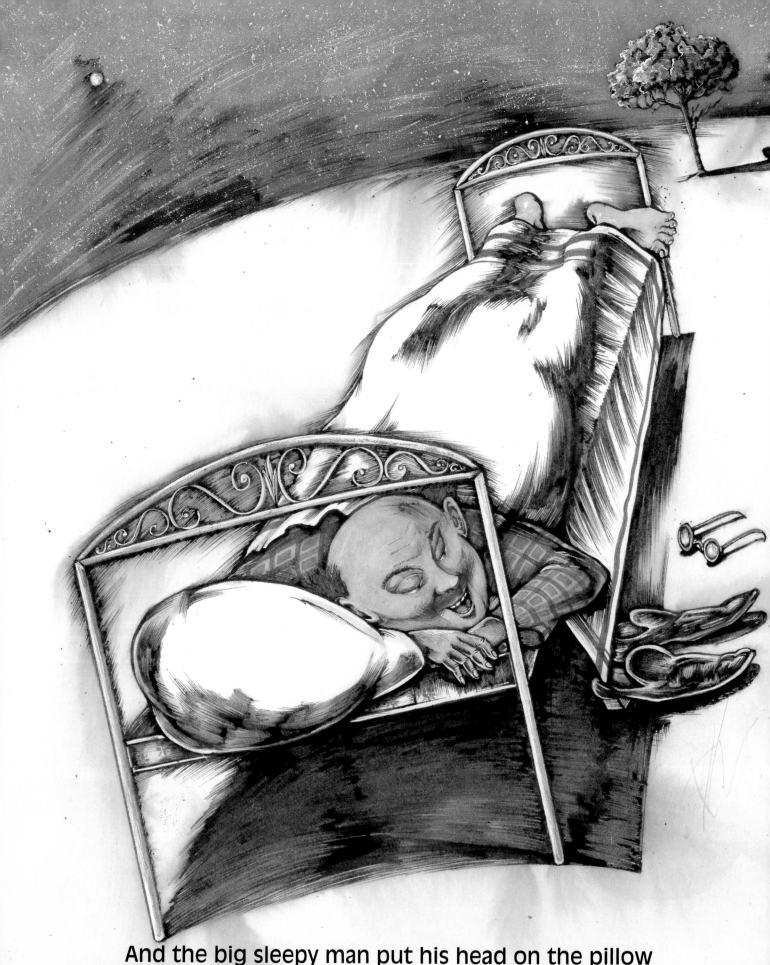

And the big sleepy man put his head on the pillow
and the little sleepy man put his head on the pillow.

And the big sleepy man sang a big sleepy song
and the little sleepy man sang a little sleepy song.

Then the big sleepy man told the little sleepy man a story
about the Man in the Moon, who was once a little boy,
not much bigger than the little
sleepy man.
And how
the little boy
Man in the Moon
got up
every night
and ran around
all night until
by daytime
he was so
hungry

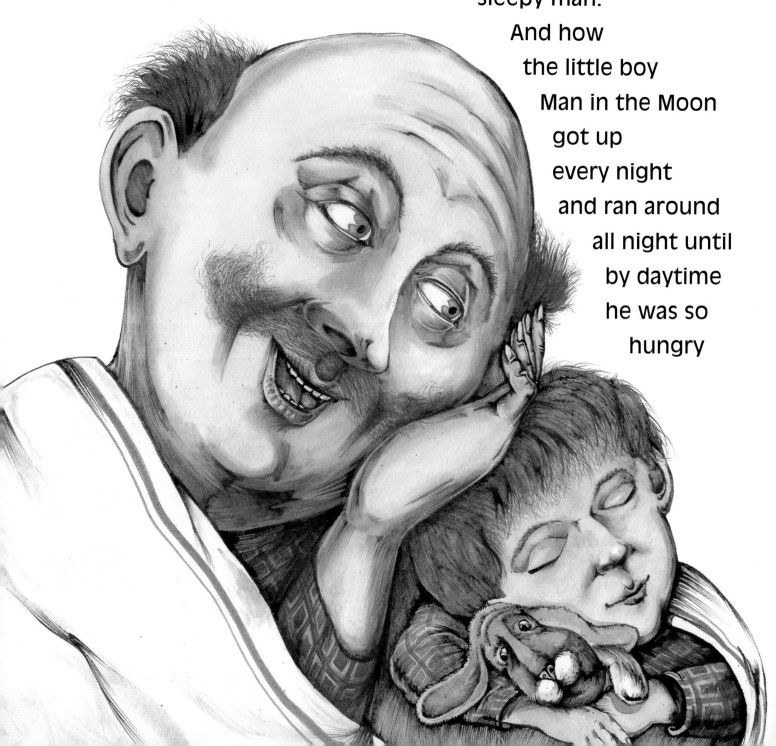

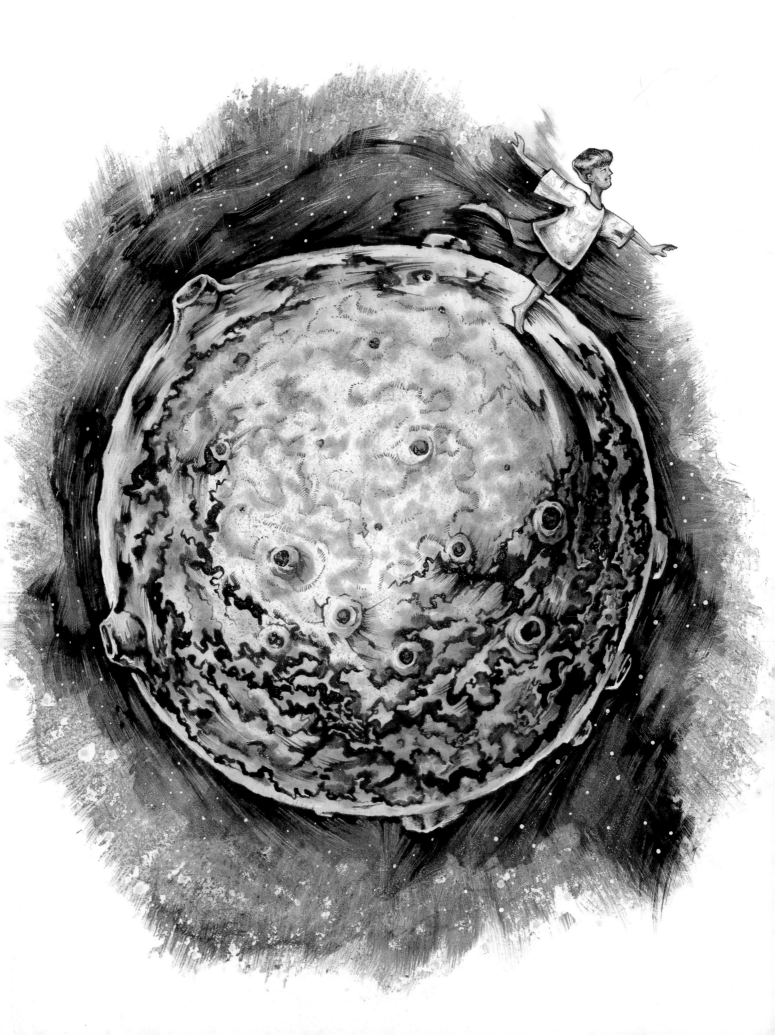

HE ATE

A BIG FAT DINNER

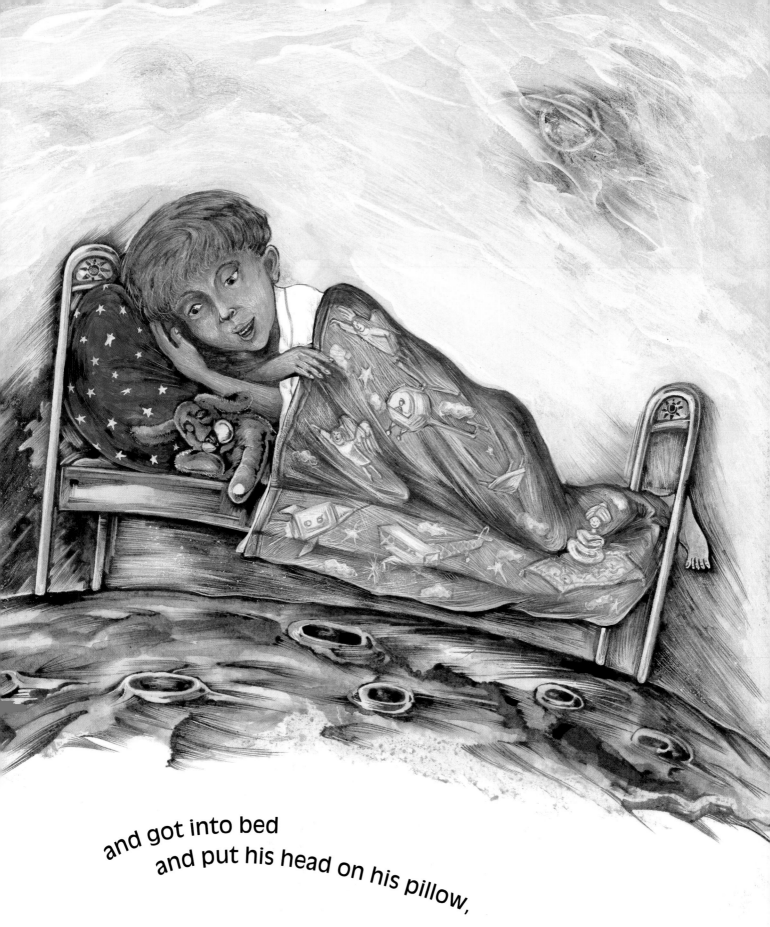

and got into bed
and put his head on his pillow,

and slowly, slowly, slowly,
and quietly, quietly, quietly,
and gently, gently, gently
he went day after day after day to sleep
and dreamed he was the Man in the Moon.

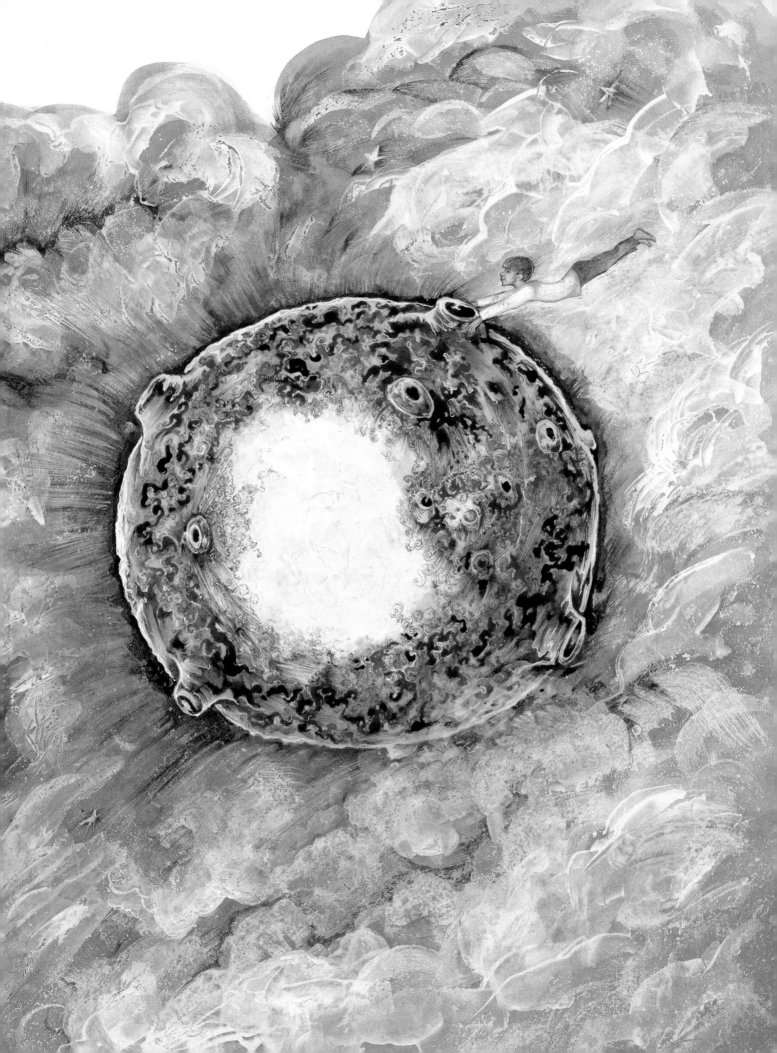

And the little sleepy man listened
and he never said a word.
But he thought about the moonlight,

and the starlight,

and the sunlight at noon,

and how he'd be sleeping pretty soon.

Then the **big** sleepy man closed his eyes
and the LITTLE sleepy man
closed his eyes.
And the little sleepy man
thought of the moon
again,
and again,
and again.

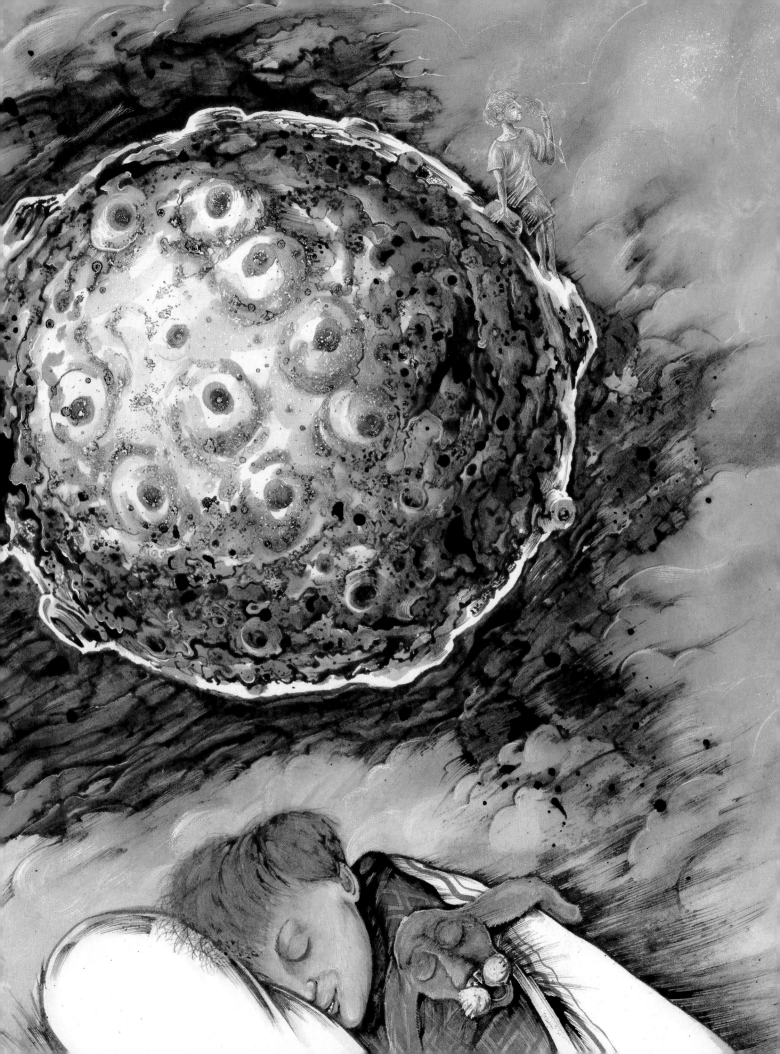

And he never said a word because he was sound asleep.